RANDY NEWMAN *harps and angels*

Cover Photo: Autumn de Wilde

Cathy Kerr Management
7715 Sunset Boulevard, Suite 100
Los Angeles, CA 90046

Arrangements supervised and edited by Michael Roth

Visit **randynewman.com**

Alfred Publishing Co., Inc.
16320 Roscoe Blvd., Suite 100
P.O. Box 10003
Van Nuys, CA 91410-0003
alfred.com

Copyright © MMVIII by Alfred Publishing Co., Inc.
All rights reserved. Printed in USA.

ISBN-10: 0-7390-5740-5
ISBN-13: 978-0-7390-5740-7

RANDY NEWMAN

On the title track of *Harps and Angels*, which opens Randy Newman's first album of all-new studio recordings since 1999's Bad Love, a man lies stricken on a New Orleans sidewalk, about to gasp his last breath. It's clearly the Crescent City, given the loose, jazzy shuffle the band is playing, Newman's languid drawl, and the *laissez faire* attitude of God himself when He appears to report that somebody up there had made a clerical error and the tearful guy on the pavement is not going to join his maker after all. That sets the tone for what follows: *Harps and Angels* boasts a deceptively easy-going quality even as it tackles matters of life and death, memory and loss, the discontents of the rich and famous, the problems of the poor, governmental malfeasance, corporate cynicism, and the veritable end of an empire — namely, our own.

The arrival of *Harps and Angels* was foreshadowed more than a year ago by a conversational number called "A Few Words In Defense of Our Country," which Newman developed during a summer 2006 tour of Europe, then slipped into his stateside sets. With a lilting country waltz as backdrop, Newman presents a caustic view of the state of our nation, ostensibly as a defense against foreign criticism. As incisive as it is darkly funny, "A Few Words in Defense of Our Country" caught the attention of *The New York Times*, which offered Newman space on its Op Ed page to print the lyrics. A wickedly effective digital single came next, including an eyebrow-raising verse about the Supreme Court that the *Times* censored. *Rolling Stone* named it one of the singles of the year, "right behind Jay-Z and ahead of Rihanna," Newman helpfully points out.

"I don't like writing songs that are right on the nose, Tom Lehrer-like songs, commenting on what's happening in the moment," Newman admits, "because songs like that will go away. This one will go away because this administration will go away, and we'll never have one quite like it. But I wanted to say something, so I did."

It turns out that Newman has a lot to say. "Piece of the Pie" is even more audacious social commentary than "A Few Words In Defense of Our Country" — a full-blown musical-theatre-style song that features orchestral backing arranged and conducted by Newman; a "patriots chorus," defending the honor of John Mellencamp for licensing a song to General Motors; and a tribute to the social consciousness of Jackson Browne. Says Newman, "It's an old-time sort of Industrial Workers of the World, socialist thing. The fact that you can work real hard and do all the country says you're supposed to do, and still not make it is a little surprising, you know what I mean? It's hard to get used to the fact that things are not getting better and better, that if you work hard and do what you're supposed to, it still might not work for you." The proceedings are briefly interrupted by a pair of bickering Belgians, proving that even the tiniest, prettiest places can be divisive.

The arrangements throughout *Harps And Angels* have a jaunty, Dixieland feel, with Newman on piano fronting a club-size combo, and he brings a touch of the blues to his vocals: "It's the way my voice sounds best to me at the moment, doing blues oriented stuff. That's the kind of singer I think I am." His orchestrations, featured on several tracks, are as gorgeous as anything he has produced on his film scores, and lend his misanthropic tales an improbably grand quality. With three of his uncles having been successful Hollywood composers, Newman says, "I grew up with maybe an inordinate love of the orchestral sound. When I was five years old, I was fifty feet away from the greatest musicians in the world, the studio guys. Guys I learned later were known worldwide. I had and still have enormous respect for my Uncle Alfred and the work he did. I'm not as good as he is with my film music – but no one else is either, so that's not something I have to worry about."

On "Laugh and Be Happy," he provides a prescription for the troubles of America's immigrant population, set to a madcap Charleston-worthy tempo. "Korean Parents" is more like an elegant ballroom dance, with kitschy Oriental embellishments; Newman takes on the sorry condition of American education by employing clichés about overachieving Asian students, and does it in such earnest fashion he's sure to offend just about everybody.

Newman contrasts the satire with a downright moving pair of ballads. "Losing You" is based on a story his physician brother recounted about a couple whose son was dying: "His parents had been in the camps during World War II. They said, we made it, we were able to get over the fact that we lost both of our families, but we don't have enough time left to get over losing our son." "Feels Like Home" is a proudly sentimental love song, a surprisingly heartwarming denouement to the album: "People are going to like 'Feels Like Home', it's going to be the most successful song on the album probably, because that's the nature of the world, even though I mostly choose a different kind of song to write, other than straight ballads. That's what people like me doing the best – songs 'Feels Like Home' or 'Marie' [from *Good Old Boys*], whereas my favorite songs are like 'Only A Girl' or 'Harps and Angels,' ones with characters, a cast, a narrator."

Harps and Angels was co-produced by Mitchell Froom and Lenny Waronker. Froom, whose credits include Crowded House, Los Lobos, and Sheryl Crow, first worked with Newman on *Bad Love* and returned for Newman's 2003 Nonesuch debut, *Songbook, Vol. 1*, voice-and-piano renderings of older, classic material. Says Newman, "Mitchell is a great musician and is enormously helpful at getting a basic track to really work. Finding a groove – that's not a word I like, but it's the only one there is. There definitely is such a thing but I wouldn't know what to tell a bass player or a drummer. Mitchell does that and he's enormously supportive in saying the right thing."

Waronker, former Warner Bros. head, is Newman's childhood buddy and life-long champion: "His instincts are better than mine, in some respects. He's always been, for me, the most crucial person to my career. When I was sixteen or seventeen, Lenny was my backbone. I was too shy to play stuff for people and he was always the first person — in the first 25 years or so of my career life — I would play things for. Lenny was always there with enthusiasm or a suggestion and a drive I didn't have myself. I wanted to be the best I could be, but Lenny wanted me to the best in the world, and I owe him a great deal."

On *Harps and Angels*, Randy Newman makes us laugh, gets us mad, cajoles us to think. He chronicles the ways we fall apart and catalogues the emotions that bring us together. Call it the soundtrack to our lives. — Michael Hill

CONTENTS

Harps and Angels 4
Losing You 14
Laugh and Be Happy 19
A Few Words in Defense of
Our Country 26
A Piece of the Pie 35
Easy Street 44
Korean Parents 51
Only A Girl 58
Potholes 74
Feels Like Home 66

HARPS AND ANGELS

Words and Music by
RANDY NEWMAN

LOSING YOU

Words and Music by
RANDY NEWMAN

Moderately slow, freely with feeling ♩ = 96

© 2008 RANDY NEWMAN MUSIC (ASCAP)
All Rights Reserved

LAUGH AND BE HAPPY

Words and Music by
RANDY NEWMAN

A FEW WORDS IN DEFENSE OF OUR COUNTRY

Words and Music by
RANDY NEWMAN

A Few Words in Defense of Our Country - 9 - 1
31931

© 2008 RANDY NEWMAN MUSIC (ASCAP)
All Rights Reserved

A PIECE OF THE PIE

Words and Music by
RANDY NEWMAN

A Piece of the Pie - 9 - 9
31931

EASY STREET

Words and Music by
RANDY NEWMAN

51

KOREAN PARENTS

Words and Music by
RANDY NEWMAN

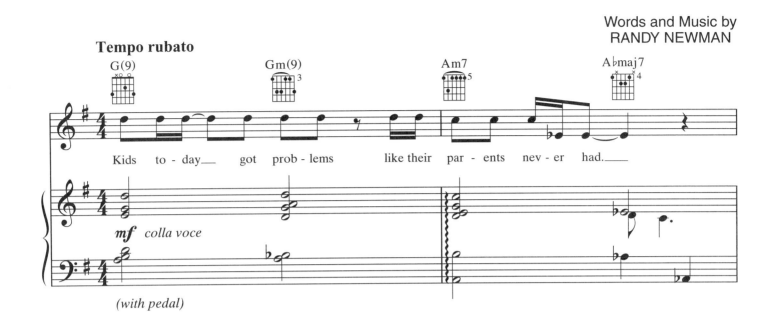
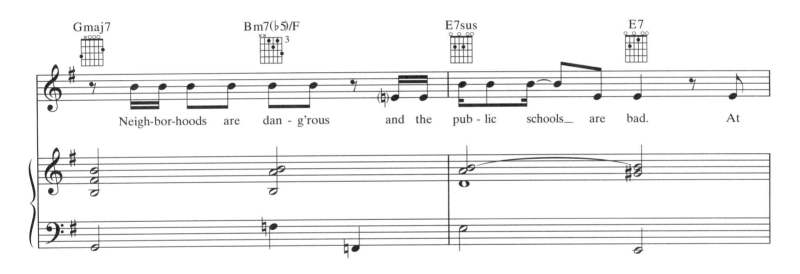
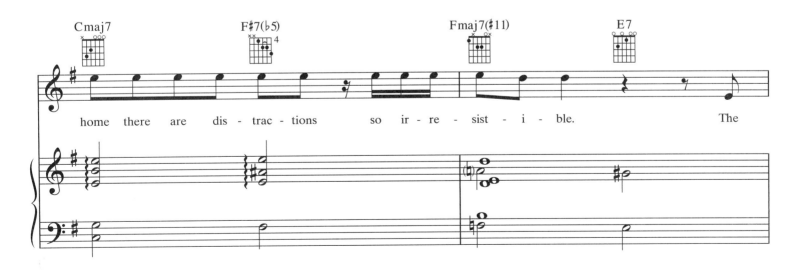

Korean Parents - 7 - 1
31931

© 2008 RANDY NEWMAN MUSIC (ASCAP)
All Rights Reserved

ONLY A GIRL

**Words and Music by
RANDY NEWMAN**

Moderately fast shuffle ♩ = 144

Verse 1:

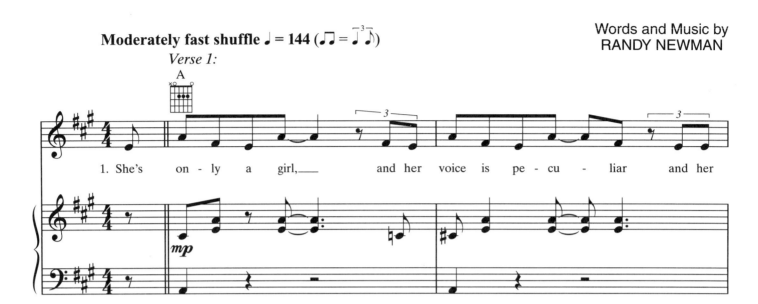

1. She's on-ly a girl, and her voice is pe-cu-liar and her

Use this r.h. lick as the feel & rhythm throughout and use the written notation as a guide to fill out the accompaniment ad lib. – play sparingly, with as light a touch as possible.

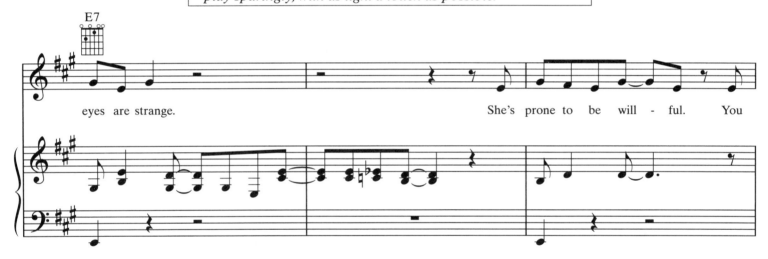

eyes are strange. She's prone to be will-ful. You

try to cheer her up some, but she's im-per-vious to change. She

© 2008 RANDY NEWMAN MUSIC (ASCAP)
All Rights Reserved

62

Only a Girl - 8 - 5
31931

FEELS LIKE HOME

Words and Music by
RANDY NEWMAN

© 2008 RANDY NEWMAN MUSIC (ASCAP)
All Rights Reserved

POTHOLES

Words and Music by
RANDY NEWMAN